Kimono

Dragon

Records

着物

オオトカゲ

記録

By: Evelyn Espinoza

ISBN: 9798842613489 (Paperback)

Any references to historical events, real people, or real places are used fictitiously. Names and characters are products of the author's imagination.

Front cover image by Evelyn Espinoza.
Book design by Evelyn Espinoza.
Original Watercolor and Pen Illustrations by Evelyn Espinoza

Summary: A Komodo Dragon tries to blend while living in Japan wearing a kimono: even the mundane is an adventure for her.

First printing edition 2022.

Independently Published

www.evelyncurryart.com

Can you tell me about 'kimono' dragons, Mamá? said my
three year old son. Of course, I said, smiling inwardly to
myself and picturing a Komodo dragon in a kimono.

Komodo Dragons
(Varanus Komodoensis)

I do not wish to alarm you, but living dragons still exist! I am referring to the
Komodo Dragon, the largest in the monitor lizard family. They rule the Indonesian
Islands hunting many creatures native to that habitat. So, take care and do not
wander around their islands alone!

With armored scaly skin, and a mighty long tail, these dragons are powerfully strong.
But wait, there's more! Not only do they have sharp teeth, but their saliva is
venomous too. And if that wasn't terrifying enough, they can run fast and cover
short distances when they chase their prey.
Oh please, let's stay out of their path! And do not forget about their huge claws,
with terrible talons, which they use most effectively to rip and to dig. Oh yes, they
are quite the picture of a living dragon!

着物 Ki-mo-no

Ki means wear, and mono means thing. The wear-thing of Japan. Kimonos come in bright and colorful patterns and styles. Some have very long sleeves. They are made of different materials like linen, silk, polyester, rayon, and cotton.

First, you wrap the kimono around you and then you tie it around your waist with a belt (obi).

Men's kimonos are usually made in solid colors such as blues, blacks, browns, and greys. Some kimonos are filled geometric patterns and shapes. Others have pictures of cranes flying over streams, mountains, or dragons and tigers! The very fancy ones have gold brocade worked into them, adorned with painted flowers, and embroidered leaves.

So, what exactly is a Kimono Dragon you ask?

着物 オオトカゲ Kimono Dragon

Let me introduce you to the Kimono Dragon. She's a demure character. She tries to blend in, but always ends up sticking out very noticeably in all sorts of situations!

She is playing her 三味線 Sha-mi-sen (three-stringed instrument) inside the 高台寺 観月台 Kou-dai-ji Kan-ge-tsu-dai (moon viewing pavilion). Outside of the round window, the bamboo leaves are fluttering in the moonlit air.

She mostly plays at night because she does not want to risk distressing anyone with her dragon-ness. Can you imagine taking an afternoon walk, enjoying the calm and peace of a Japanese garden, and suddenly you stumble upon a dragon?! Even though she is in a kimono and behaving herself, it would still be quite a sight!

But she is respectful and does not want to alarm anyone, so she keeps her Sha-mi-sen playing during moonlit nights, entertaining the owls, the frogs, and the crickets alike.

餅つき Mo-chi-tsu-ki 祭り Ma-tsu-ri

Our Kimono Dragon has been invited to a 餅 mo-chi making festival. I suspect her strong shoulders and powerful arms have something to do with it. Mo-chi pounding takes muscles! And Komodo Dragons have lots of muscles! She isn't wearing her kimono today. Instead, a winter puffer jacket and warm pants are much more suitable for pounding hot rice.

The man next to her quickly turns the rice over in between each mallet swing. They both work together in perfect timing and with great trust. After a while, the rice becomes sticky and shiny. It is ready to have sweet filling added to it, and then it is rolled into a little ball.

I like my mo-chi with fresh strawberries inside. How would you like yours? Sweet bean paste is delicious, too. The ladies at the tables are making some sweet bean-paste filled mo-chi for the festival.

There is also hot dai-kon (white radish) soup to warm yourself up on this cold winter day. Our Kimono Lady would also recommend pounding the rice with the mallet to keep warm. She has worked up quite an appetite.

節分 Se-tsu-bun

節分 Se-tsu-bun is at the beginning of February and
it is the last day of Winter. It is a tradition to throw roasted
soybeans or 福豆 Fuku-mame (fortune beans) at the o-ni (demon/ogre). This will get
rid of the last year's bad spirits, and to prepare for the new year.

Our Kimono Dragon is at a temple in Tokyo. But wait, what's this? Oh no! In her
unique greenness, she has been mistaken for an o-ni! And there is no time to explain
that she is not wearing a mask! This is the face she was born with! She joins priests
and gei-sha on stage, along with many o-ni masked characters.

She is given a red box filled with roasted soybeans. She throws them to the crowds of
people with outstretched hands. They scramble to catch all the soybeans they can to
get good luck in the new year! Nobody seems to notice that our Dragon friend has
the green claws to go with her green face. She has a very good costume, they may
conclude.

Before long, our Dragon lady is enjoying herself and forgets that
she resembles a scary looking o-ni! She leaves the temple
munching on roasted soybeans.

You should try them too because they are very good for you;
high in protein, and also in fiber.

ラーメン Ra-a-men

It is time for some dinner. Let's stop at a little 'hole-in-the- wall' Ra-a-men restaurant. It is very small with only a few seats. But there is enough space for her if she keeps her tail tucked in!

How do you think our Kimono Dragon gets on with chopsticks? I suspect she has spent many hours at home perfecting the handling chopsticks with her massive claws.

Do you hear that? If you lean in closely, I dare say you can hear her slurping her Ra-a-men with satisfaction! This is a customary way to eat Ra-a-men: no one would turn around to question the loud slurps; no frowns of disgust.

She is enjoying a rich, creamy broth topped with various types of mushrooms, one boiled egg, and のり No-ri (dried seaweed).

なると Na-ru-to slices adorn the Ra-a-men, which is seasoned fish paste. Na-ru-to might not sound very delicious, but it looks and tastes like imitation crab sticks.

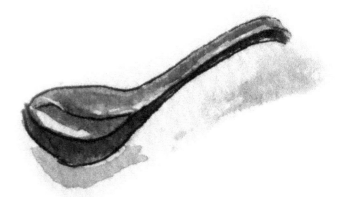

Picnic Time

It's finally Spring and that means picnic time! Our Kimono Dragon rides her bicycle to the '7-11' convenience store for some picnic worthy snacks. Look at what she has selected. Please bear in mind that it's not all for her! She has bought enough to share with her friends.

She has bottles of milk tea and lemon tea, egg-filled sandwiches dressed in creamy Japanese mayonnaise between thick, soft white bread. She also has sweet メロンパン Melon Ball bread, and おにぎり O-ni-gi-ri (triangles of rice filled with pork, salmon, or tuna fillings covered in No-ri. Our dragon's favorites are the tuna mayonnaise filled o-ni-gi-ri and the soft-boiled eggs.

For dessert there's some 花見 Ha-na-mi 団子 Dan-go, or three flavored mo-chi balls on a stick. I doubt she can eat them one at a time in a refined manner. No, they are too scrumptious! She gobbles up all three at once! There are pillowy soft white bread sandwiches filled with custard and whipped cream holding plump strawberry slices in place. This will be a picnic to remember.

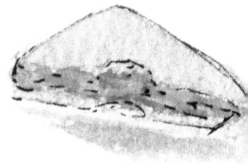

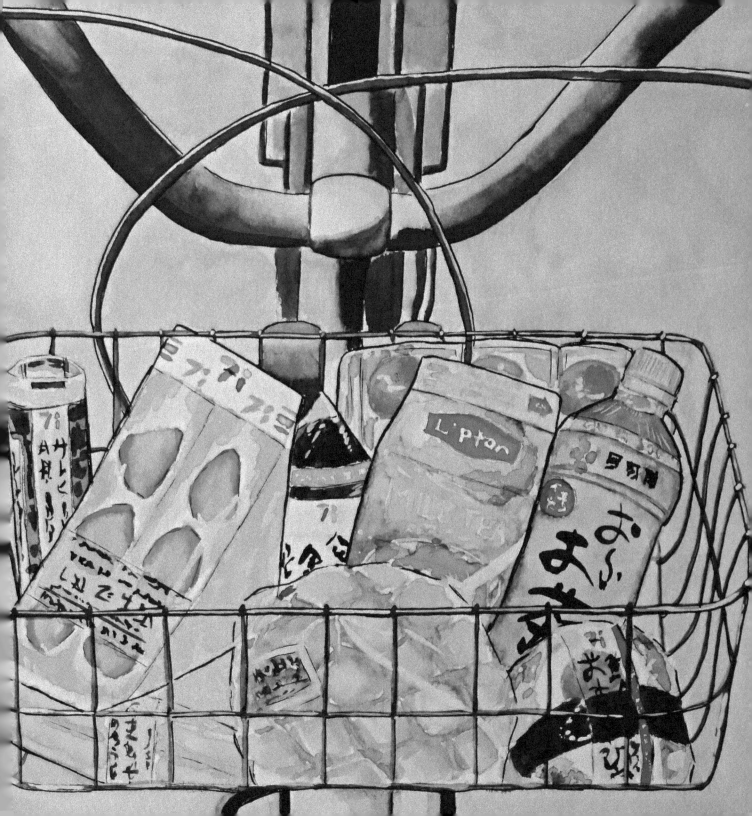

花見 Ha-na-mi

The さくら Sa-ku-ra (cherry blossoms) are in full bloom. We follow our Dragon friend down to the river. She propped her bike up against a nearby tree. Have you imagined how our Kimono Dragon rides her bike? I wonder what she does with that tail of hers.

We find her enjoying the company of her friends, but they are not Komodo Dragons. By now, you may be wondering if our Kimono Dragon has other dragon friends. It's possible they might join her in another adventure.

Only the locals know about this beautiful spot. Now, it is time to relax and enjoy the blossoms blooming 花見 Ha-na-mi. Families and friends have spread their blue tarps on the new Spring grass under the flower-filled trees. The smell of picnic treats fills the air trying to outdo the Sa-ku-ra perfume.

We can also hear laughter and chatting. We can see people napping. We can listen to children splashing in the stream. Other people take afternoon strolls under the canopy of blossoms. Birds sing as they flit from branch to branch.

Tulips and Cameras

昭和記念公園 Sho-wa Ki-nen Park is the largest park in the Tokyo area. It used to be a Japanese military airbase.

Just so you know, Show-a Ki-ne-n Park is the place to go to regardless of the season. Even in the winter, it is beautiful! Today it is Spring, and we are wandering through the tulip garden. Show-a Ki-ne-n Park has a wonderful tulip garden. It almost looks like you are walking through a rainbow. There is every color of tulip to be enjoyed, even dark purple ones. It gets very busy during tulip season.

The tulips are sensational, but it is more interesting to watch all the photographers. They bring large tripods to hold even larger cameras with even longer lenses to photograph the rainbow sea of tulips.

There are as many photographers as there are tulips! Every few feet, there is a head atop with a hat and a camera poking out of the rows of tulips.

Artists set up their easels, striving to copy the tulip colors they see. Even our Kimono Dragon is among the flower beds taking pictures of the tulips with her large camera. Would you say she has blended in yet?

On The Train

Many people wear face masks while traveling in trains. This helps to keep your germs away from other people; especially if you have a cough or a cold, and if you still must go to work or to school. The train is usually crowded.

The man is so tired, his head drops onto our Kimono Dragon's shoulder. He must have had a long day at work and a long train journey. Our Kimono lady sits there patiently awaiting her stop, looking out the window thinking of things other than a stranger's head upon her shoulder.

Even though there are lots of passengers on the train, it is quiet. Passengers avoid eating and talking on the phone as it may disturb other passengers. No annoying crunching of carrots or smelling a pungent pickle sandwich. Even music on headphones is kept to a quiet, personal-hearing level.

Some commuters read to pass the time. Books are usually covered to give the reader some privacy as to what they are reading, and to keep the book clean and protected from wear and tear. Everyone is respectful of each other, because of having little personal space wherever you go in public places. But you get used to it after a while.

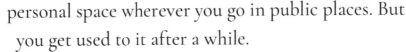

A Trip to the Zoo

Visiting the zoo, we find our Kimono Dragon at the Komodo Dragon enclosure. This is quite an amusing sight! Do you think the Komodo dragons notice one of their own kind outside of the enclosure? Perhaps they wonder: "How did she get out?!" After all she is behaving very unlike a Komodo dragon dressed in a summer kimono, or 浴衣 Yu-ka-ta.

One of the large lizards looks puzzled, cocking its reptilian head to one side. One isn't bothered at all and continues waddling along sticking out its long, forked tongue.

And how does our Dragon Lady respond? Does it make her miss her home in Indonesia? Even in a Yu-ka-ta, she's still a large green dragon.

The other zoo visitors don't seem to notice that one of the Komodo dragons are not in the enclosure. The carry on photographing the zoo exhibits. Perhaps they don't want to point it out and risk possibly embarrassing our Dragon friend.

Sunday Chores

Today is Sunday. After attending church, our Dragon lady has spent the rest of the day at home, resting and catching up. Sunday seems to be a popular day to hang the washing out and to air out the 掛け布団 (かけぶとん) ka-ke-bu-to-n (duvet) on the balconies. Our Kimono Dragon has her washing line on the rooftop of her little green house.

I remember walking around this part of Tokyo and discovering this little green house. Of course, our Kimono Dragon lives here. It's green. It's perfect!

You can see that her home doesn't have much of a garden. Personal living space is limited everywhere. So, she tends her many potted plants on her balcony and in front of her house. It's easy to lose sight of where her plants end, and her neighbors' plants begin!

Today, we find her watering the plants. She must move around carefully up there as the plant pots fill the rooftop, but her tail does get in the way occasionally knocking over a pot or two. Look out below!

Wisteria

Towards the end of April and beginning of May, the
heavenly aromas of the wisteria fill the air. At
A-shi-ka-ga Flower Park, there are many wisteria
tunnels carefully groomed to grow over into
beautiful arches. These give perfect shade from the
sun making the stroll under the arch wonderfully
relaxing. Old, old trees weighed down with pink, white,
yellow, purple flowers. Perfumed blossoms.

It's a good day to enjoy wisteria-flavored ice cream. What
do you think it tastes like? Wisteria flowers smell sweet and floral and a little
musky. Now those scents don't sound as though they would taste nice, but trust
me, it works in the ice cream. Imagine if a flower tasted as good as it smelled.
That's a little bit how wisteria-flavored ice cream tastes like. I hope you can try it
one day.

Oh no! While I was describing the ice cream, our Kimono Dragon friend
couldn't wait and gobbled hers up! It was so good, and her dragon tongue
is made to eat ice cream very quickly. She will have to get a another
one, but this time she had better make sure she savors the
moment.

鯉のぼり Koi-no-bo-ri

Today is May 5th which means it is National Children's Day. Throughout the month, local establishments hang up colorful carp streamers in honor of children.

The Koi-no-bo-ri are hung to bring children good luck and so they may grow up to be healthy and strong. Children enjoy not having to go to school today, and the parents enjoy not having to go to work: it's a national holiday!

At Tokyo Tower, hundreds of rows of fluttering Koi-no-bo-ri are hung up surrounding the tower. The wind makes them dance all day. It's a beautiful rainbow to stand under.

Our Kimono Dragon has made a special trip to the tower to stand under these carp streamers. It is a holiday, which means it is terribly busy everywhere. But surprisingly the tourists and visitors give our Kimono Dragon plenty of space. She makes use of this space by taking selfies and enjoying the wind-blown fluttering carp streamers of the Koi-no-bo-ri.

Shibuya Crossing

Shibuya Crossing is always extremely busy. It's not called the busiest crosswalk in the world for nothing! Rainy days are no exception. You can watch a sea of moving people in all directions, while the little green man flashes on crosswalks. They look like little moving mushrooms from up here.

The transparent plastic umbrellas are the most popular because you can actually see where you're walking. Even cyclists use umbrellas in the rain on their bike. It is difficult to spot the person who does not have their umbrella. I can only presume that everyone takes an umbrella with them regardless of whether it's raining or not.

The humid summertime usually brings lots of rain with it. For the people who do forget to take an umbrella, they can always find them at most convenient stores.

Even though our Kimono Dragon blends in with the crowd with her own transparent plastic umbrella, she sticks out with her dragon-ness! I wonder how she keeps her tail from getting all wet and dirty. Does she wipe it on the doormat along with her feet before she enters a building?

Bicycles

Crossing the street with children can be quite the adventure. You can see our Kimono Dragon crossing the street. She is on her bicycle with her two little children. The youngest Komodo Dragon boy waves to the driver. I am quite positive the driver will remember this crossing for a while! They are on their way to the playground.

You also see a group of children crossing the road but walking the opposite way. They must be heading home from school at this time of day. Do you notice how they raise their hand when crossing the road? Children are taught to do this as part of road safety, so car drivers can see them better. This is very useful, particularly for the shorter children.

You can see the driver in this car waits patiently. I hope no one gets distracted by the Komodo Dragon family riding a bicycle, since I suspect it is an unusual sight.

七夕 (たなばた) Ta-na-ba-ta

The Ta-na-ba-ta Festival happens during the months of July and August. It is a tradition to write your wishes on a bamboo tree with the hope they will come true. What might you wish for? I wonder what the Komodo Dragon family wished for.

The brightly colored written wishes hang restlessly in the branches of bamboo. Large, colorful streamers hang throughout the streets, and dancers perform at various times throughout the day.

The air is humid with crowds of people wandering about leisurely. There are lots of street vendors selling food and there are many games to play. Children wear their colorful patterned Yu-ka-tas.

Our Kimono Dragon and her family leisurely walk around enjoying the festivities while sharing snacks. Gorgeous firework displays fill the tepid night sky. Don't forget: Find your place early, as the parks get very crowded!

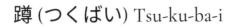

蹲 (つくばい) Tsu-ku-ba-i

On this trip, our Kimono Dragon visits a temple. First, she stops at the つくばい Tsu-ku-ba-i (the wash basin) for ceremonial cleansing before entering.

It is a hot and humid day, so she does need to freshen up. She pours water from the bamboo cup over her claws. Once her claws are clean, she fills the cup again and has a little drink. But not from the cup directly; that would be unhygienic! She pours the water into her cleansed hands and slurps it up.

Do you think the girls on the red bridge have noticed our Dragon Lady? Probably not. I suspect they are too busy taking photos of themselves in their pretty Yu-ka-tas.

Visitors are enjoying peaceful strolls under the pine trees and bamboo forest.

相撲 Su-mo-u

This is a grand event which happens in the months of February and September. Our Kimono Dragon has a good seat close to the arena. However, she does not want to be too close just in case the competitors fall out of the ring and land on her! Occasionally, this does happen, and I can tell you I would not want to be breaking the fall of any 300lbs Sumo wrestler! No, thank you!

The front seats are filled with photographers furiously clicking away. There is a great deal of ritual preparation before the fight begins; lots of stretching and bowing. Salt is thrown in to cleanse the ring. Sumo wrestlers intimidate each other with their belly slapping, thigh slapping, arm slapping; lots of slapping. Sometimes they slap their thighs to get the salt off their hands, but most of it is to intimidate their opponent.

We wait. They charge. They grab and grapple each other. And as quickly as it started, it is over. My, wasn't that thrilling? Won't you stay to watch the next match?

Vending Machines

Our Kimono Dragon is back in Tokyo.
She has been walking around, hopping on
and off trains and shopping all day.

She is thirsty. She finds a convenient group of vending machines in a convenient location along the street. Which drink shall she choose from to refresh herself? Do you think she'll buy a hot beverage marked in red? Maybe some hot corn chowder in a can? I think I'll never want to try that! Warming, sweet milk tea? No, this Autumn weather is still too warm for hot drinks. She wants cooling refreshment. So, blue marked drinks it is! She is going to buy some chilled lemon tea, probably two bottles. Dragons get very thirsty. I just hope her claws are not too big to get the drink out of the vending machine.

When she is done drinking it, she will put her PET bottle in the correct recycling bin. There is always a convenient recycling bin next to the convenient vending machines. Dare I overuse the word, but isn't that convenient?

温泉 On-sen

These are lovely, relaxing public bath houses. Before getting into the hot, clean water, our Kimono Dragon washes herself first. She is sharing the water with other people, so she must be clean first. How awful would it be if she got in the on-sen with soap suds still on her, or worse, if she got in unwashed?! She would be asked to leave, of course!

So, our Kimono Dragon uses her little towel and plenty of soap to wash herself. Scaly armored skin takes some diligent scrubbing. That little towel is then folded up and placed on her head while she's in the water.

Our Dragon Lady closes her eyes as she submerges herself in the relaxing, hot water. The warm Autumn breeze brings the forest scent through this on-sen. She doesn't want to draw too much attention to herself, so she makes it a point to keep her tail close to her. She doesn't wish to take up too much room, but it is not very crowded in the pool.

The other ladies keep their eyes to themselves and are polite and respectable about a dragon joining them.

神社 Shrine 骨董 Ko-tto-u 蚤の市 No-mi-no-i

This is essentially a flea market, a rummage sale, or a car boot sale. They take place within shrin courtyards. Will you pass by some overpriced junk? Or will you find a rare treasure for a barg Usually haggling or bargaining is not considered polite, but at a shrine sale it is tolerated. Many antique wares are for sale. But you must show up very early for the good deals!

You will find tea pots and tea sets, pottery, sake cups, glass fishing floats, books, Kimonos, Yukatas, and colorful and decorative embroidered O-bi (belt/sash), 小芥子 Ko-ke-shi Dolls (a traditional doll for children to play with), household goods, toys, collectibles, and memorabilia.

Our Kimono Dragon has bought some woodblock prints, and a couple of large Kimonos to fit her large dragon size. She is also looking for some 浮き玉 U-ki-da-ma fishing floats made of glass to decorate her small fishpond at her home (sadly, the fish packed up and left; they were too scared of her dragon face peering down into the water). She haggled and bargained just enough to keep within the side of politeness. Is it possible she used her naturally fierce expression to help lower the final agreed upon price?

干し柿 Ho-shi-ga-ki

Persimmon hanging occurs during the Autumn when it is still warm and sunny, but the humidity has left until next Summer.

Our Kimono Dragon is visiting some of her friends who live in the countryside. She is helping them to hang their harvested persimmons to dry in the Autumn sun.

She ties each fruit with string and loops it over the bamboo pole. She uses her large claws deftly to tie neat knots around the persimmon stems. She is not clumsy at all. How painstaking it must be to tie and hang all those persimmons! But, oh, how symmetrically beautiful they look glowing in the sun like bright amber.

Have you eaten fresh persimmons? They are deliciously sweet, with a taste that reminds me a little bit like cinnamon. But I must admit I have not tried a dried persimmon ever before. I'm sure it is very good though.

Try adding them to your hot tea for some sweetness. Also, enjoy a chewy, sweet, dried persimmon snack during the winter months.

酒 Sake with 芸者 Ge-i-sha

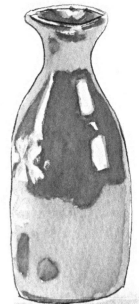

Our Kimono Dragon has gone to a guest house at Mount Ta-ka-o. She has enjoyed an evening of amusing performances, fun games, and eloquent dancing by 芸者Ge-i-sha (entertainer) and 舞妓 Mai-ko (apprentice Gei-sha).

We observe her chatting with the Gei-sha while they pour our Kimono Dragon some sake (fermented rice alcohol drink). The tiny sake cup is held very carefully by our friend's large green claws. It would be so easy for her to snap it into several pieces, but she has great restraint.

They look to be having a good time. What might they be talking about? What does a Gei-sha have in common with a Kimono Dragon, you ask? Kimonos!

Some exquisitely presented appetizers accompany the sake and conversation. Seasonal treats are in the shape of autumn leaves, with lovely flavors of chestnut and maple. It is almost a shame to eat them but having conversation with a Gei-sha makes a Kimono Dragon hungry.

Grocery Shopping

Everyone must do grocery shopping, even when they don't feel well. Our Dragon Lady has a bit of a head cold, so she is wearing a mask. No one, I repeat no one wants to be near a Komodo Dragon when they sneeze. To put it delicately, it is downright horrendous!

It is a busy day at the Daiei and the queue is long. The cashier works so quickly scanning groceries; out of one basket and into the next. It's time to pay. No one seems to acknowledge our Dragon Lady fumbling with payment due to her big claws as she tries to hit the correct buttons on the touch screen. But she is self-conscious and blushes a brighter shade of green; "ごめんなさい Go-me-n Na-sa-i" (I am sorry). Thankfully, her mask hides her embarrassment.

The cashier ignores our Dragon Lady's flustered manner, and hands her the card back with a bow and a smile, thanking her for shopping at the Daiei.

Then, our Dragon Lady will take her basket and bag her own groceries over on another side table, out of the way of other customers. She has her cloth and reusable bags. This way, there is no paying extra for plastic bags. Our Dragon Lady is environmentally friendly.

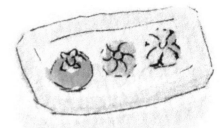

紅葉 狩り Mo-mi-ji-ga-ri

Autumn is the season for enjoying the changing colors of the Maple leaves. The afternoon sun brings a dazzling beauty to the ruby red leaves. There are areas of fiery oranges and yellows, and still some green leaves among all the red.

Our Dragon Lady has spent the day walking through the Maple Corridor row of trees with her son. They have been taking pictures of the trees, perusing through a festival market and craft fair. Now they are tired. The Autumn evening is chilly, but our Kimono Dragon doesn't mind it as she sips the warm Jasmine tea. Her son slurps his tea with enthusiasm, possibly too much enthusiasm. They enjoy some Mo-chi and seasonal treats to accompany their tea: roasted sweet potato pieces, maple and chestnut flavored 饅頭（まんじゅう）Ma-n-ju (little steamed cakes).

The big, blue, and ever-present Mt. Fuji has his winter snow hat on. This café is a peaceful spot for enjoying the beauty of the Autumn season down by Lake Ka-wa-gu-chi-ko.

The evenings are getting chilly. Her son will wander down to the lake's shore to explore one more time before the setting sun takes the light away for the day.

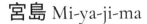

宮島 Mi-ya-ji-ma

People visit Mi-ya-ji-ma Island during all seasons, even in the Winter. There are very few people walking around the temple. It doesn't usually snow this much near Hi-ro-shi-ma, but it is very beautiful.

Our Kimono Dragon has wrapped herself up very well to view the great 鳥居 To-ri-i gate in the snow. She stands in 厳島 神 I-tsu-ku-shi-ma Shrine taking photos of the large floating red gate. Do you think her poor tail is cold? Our Kimono Lady should find someone to make her a warm, cozy snood for it!

To-ri-i gates are often found at Shinto shrines. To-ri-i means 'where the bird is.' When the tide is low, you can walk out to the large gate. Today, the gate appears to be floating on the white snow.

Mi-ya-ji-ma Island boasts of plenty head bowing and almost-tamed wild deer. Bow to the deer, and the deer bows back! However, our Kimono Dragon would argue a different story. One deer discourteously reached its head into her bag to swipe some snacks! Our Dragon Lady reprimanded the deer severely with a terrifying Komodo glare! The frightened deer remembered its manners and bounded away, bowing humbly.

And now we must say farewell to our Kimono Dragon. She doesn't quite fit in, but that doesn't seem to stop her having adventures, and I'm certain she shall have many more!

The End

Kimono 着物

Dragon オオトカゲ

Records 記録

By: Evelyn Espinoza

When my three-year-old son asked me to tell him about 'kimono' dragons, I couldn't help but suppress a smile and proceed to tell him all about Komodo dragons. But the idea of a Komodo dragon in a kimono sparked my imagination and our Kimono Lady developed.

Living in different countries, and within different cultures, has opened some unique and wonderful experiences for me. I, myself, do not fully fit into any one specific culture as I am not entirely American and not completely English. It is interesting for me to discover that often the places I ought to feel at home, I have not. Looking back through my own records, I always stood out while living in South Korea and Japan, as often I did in Portugal, Germany, and Italy. What was surprising to me was (sometimes) not feeling like I fit in within England or the United States of America. I realized I enjoy having a somewhat "celebrity-like" status wherever I go. I believe the 'not belonging' feeling became my constant, so because of it I felt as though I did belong after all.

After many travels, I find that pieces of me were left behind in each country. Perhaps that is why I get such pangs of homesickness for South Korea's mountain hikes and Springtime azaleas. I still miss a countryside ramble in England and walking through the little streets of an Italian village or stumbling upon an evening festival in Terceira. I enjoyed every minute of living in Japan – apart from that one time of me getting miserably lost in the underground ring road of downtown Tokyo and losing the GPS signal to get me out and onto the correct road home!

In my adapting and sojourning through countries, I realize that this world has such beauty to experience and that our time here is short. To conclude, we all strive to fit in and belong somewhere. But it is only when we accept that we are created by God and belong to Him, do we also realize that home is ultimately with Him, completely.

As you go out and into the world to pursue your own travels, make your own adventures, and write down your own records, remember that God will always be with you. So, grab your Kimono; pack up some persimmons and Mochi, gather up some bottles of chilled lemon tea, bring your large camera, and away we go!

Evelyn Espinoza follows our Kimono Dragon around Japan, recording her adventures through pictures and words, so she cannot really call herself an author. Most days we find Evelyn being a military wife, a mother to two boys whom she homeschools, but always an artist! Evelyn currently lives in on the white sand beaches of the Floridian Emerald Coast. She enjoys reading, painting, taking photographs, and of course, going on adventures!

CPSIA information can be obtained
at www.ICGtesting.com
Printed in the USA
BVHW021339251122
652760BV00007B/400

9 781087 981802